Here's what kids, parents, and grandparents have to say to Ron Roy, author of the  series:

"I like your books so much I can't keep my eyes off them."—Seth R.

"My sister and I love when my mother reads your mysteries. We try to guess the mystery but never can!" —Monica S.

"The map in front of the book makes me feel like I am in the story, living in Green Lawn."—Ben J.

"My favorite character is Josh, because he's so mischievous and you never know what he's going to do next."—Erica F.

"I feel like I could take out 15 A to Z Mysteries!"—Maggie K.

"I am so thrilled that my son has finally found books that are on his reading level that hold his interest. You've really made a difference in our house."—Kristin W.

"What a gift you have, Mr. Roy. You empower young children with the love of reading."—Jeanette B.

ISBN 0-439-44464-0

Text copyright © 2002 by Ron Roy.
Illustrations copyright © 2002 by John Steven Gurney.
All rights reserved. Published by Scholastic Inc., 557 Broadway, New York, NY 10012,
by arrangement with Random House Children's Books, a division of Random House, Inc.,
A TO Z MYSTERIES® is a registered trademark of Random House, Inc.
The A TO Z MYSTERIES® colophon is a registered trademark of Random House, Inc.
SCHOLASTIC and associated logos are trademarks and/or registered trademarks of Scholastic Inc.

24 23 22 21 20 19 18 17 16 15 14 13   7/0

Printed in the U.S.A.   40

First Scholastic printing, May 2003

A to Z Mysteries

The Quicksand Question

by Ron Roy

illustrated by
John Steven Gurney

SCHOLASTIC INC.

New York   Toronto   London   Auckland   Sydney
Mexico City   New Delhi   Hong Kong   Buenos Aires

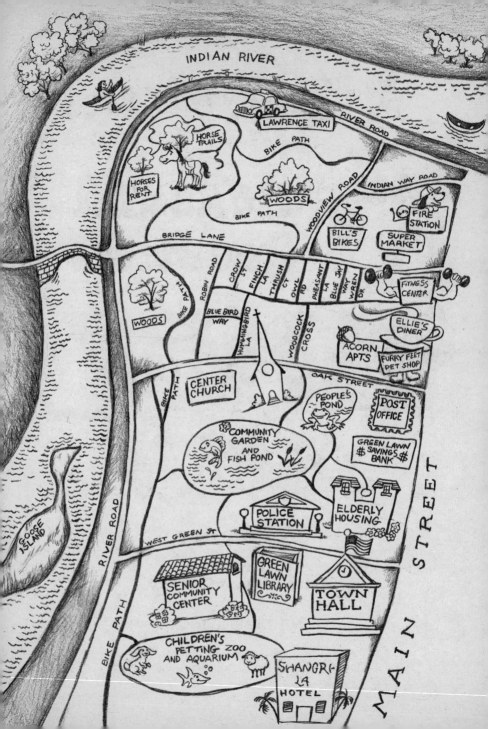

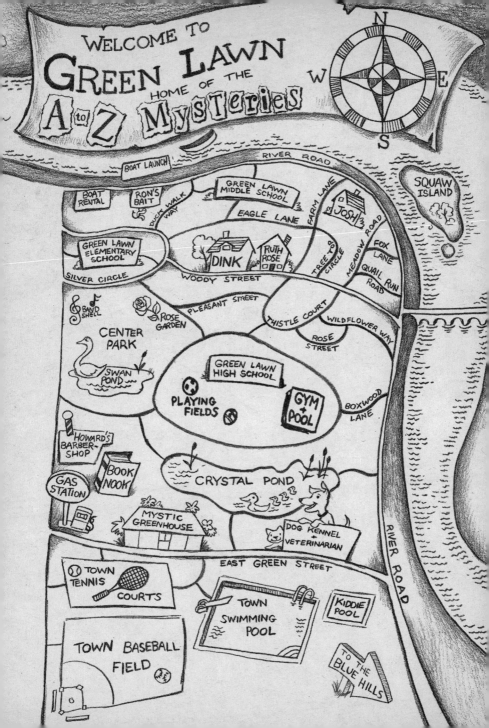

CHAPTER 1

It was Saturday night. Dink, Josh, and Ruth Rose were having a sleep-over in Josh's barn.

Dink tipped a jarful of coins onto his sleeping bag. "I can't believe the duck bank is nearly full," he said.

"I know," Ruth Rose said, emptying her piggy bank. "We've been saving for a whole year!"

"Quiet, you two," Josh said, stacking nickels, dimes, and quarters on his sleeping bag. "I can't count if you're talking!"

The "duck bank" was a large plastic bank, shaped like a duck, that stood in the fire station on Main Street. It was four feet tall and made of clear plastic. Everyone in town had been dropping money into it. They were going to use the money to pay for a special bridge just for ducks.

For years, mother ducks had been crossing River Road to build nests in the woods near Bridge Lane. After their ducklings were born, the mother ducks would lead their ducklings back across the road to the river.

The problem was, the little ducks were hard to see. Many drivers had almost had accidents. Finally, the town held a meeting to decide what to do.

One person suggested hiring a duck crossing guard.

A man who had almost driven off

the road wanted the ducks rounded up and put in cages.

Another person suggested digging a tunnel under River Road.

But a girl from Dink's school had the best idea. "My grandparents feed ducks in their yard in Florida," she'd explained. "The ducks have to cross a busy street, so my grandfather built a little bridge. My grandmother sprinkled corn on the bridge to let the ducks know it was for them. Now the ducks use the bridge all the time."

Everyone loved the idea.

Mr. Plank, the shop teacher at the high school, raised his hand. "The kids in my class can design the bridge," he said. "When we've collected enough money, I'll help them build it."

Now the bank was nearly full. On Monday morning the money would be counted by Mr. Fiskell, the president of the Green Lawn Savings Bank. As soon as school let out next week, Mr. Plank and the high school kids would start building the bridge.

Josh finished counting his money. "Nine dollars and ten cents," he said. He rubbed his stomach. "Money makes me hungry!" He grabbed his backpack and pulled out a tin of chocolate chip cookies. He also had some apples, carrots, and dog biscuits.

In her stall, Polly the pony lay sleeping on a pile of hay. Josh's dog,

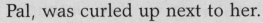

Pal, was curled up next to her.

Outside, June crickets were chirping in the field behind the barn.

"I've got ten dollars and twenty-two cents," Dink said. "What about you, Ruth Rose?"

"Fourteen dollars and thirty cents," Ruth Rose said. "How much do you suppose is in the duck bank?"

Ruth Rose liked to wear all one color. Tonight her outfit matched her sleeping bag: she wore lime green shorts and T-shirt.

"A lot," Josh said. "It's up to the duck's neck. And the three of us are putting in over *thirty* dollars!"

He opened the tin of cookies, took two for himself, and passed the rest to Ruth Rose.

"We should think of a name for the bridge," he said. "How about Waddle Way?" He kicked off his sneakers and slipped into his sleeping bag.

Dink switched off his flashlight. "What about calling it Duck Drive?"

"How about Critter Crossing?" Ruth Rose said.

"I like that," Dink said, yawning.

Josh shut off his flashlight. He snorted. "Critter Crossing, Ruth Rose? Gee, why not call it Bunny Bridge?"

Ruth Rose laughed in the dark barn. "Critter Crossing is good because other animals might use the bridge," she said. "Bunnies, turtles, raccoons. . . ."

"Buffalo," Josh added.

After a few minutes, the kids drifted off to sleep. Polly whinnied softly in her stall. Pal snored on his pile of hay.

Much later, something woke Dink. He sat up in his sleeping bag. Next to him, Josh and Ruth Rose were only lumps in the darkness.

Then Dink heard Polly stamp her hooves. When his eyes adjusted, he could see that the white pony was standing. Pal was awake, too.

Dink crawled out of his sleeping bag and walked over to the animals. He stroked Polly's warm nose. "What is it, girl?" he whispered.

Polly snorted and shook her mane. Dink knelt and scratched Pal behind his ears. "Bet you just had a bad dream," he murmured.

Using his flashlight, Dink checked his watch. It was one o'clock, and he was wide awake. He pushed the barn door open and walked outside.

The night was warm and quiet. Even the crickets were asleep. Josh's house was dark except for a small light over the back door.

Dink took a deep breath. The air smelled like the lawn had just been mowed. The springy grass felt cool under his bare feet. He yawned, stretched, and walked around the barn.

Behind the barn was a broad meadow. Next to the meadow was River Road, and on the other side of that was Indian River. On a sunny day, you could see the light glinting off the river. But now the meadow, the road, and the river were covered in darkness.

Dink was about to go back inside when he noticed two dots of light in the distance.

Car headlights, he thought. *What's a car doing in the meadow?*

Then the lights disappeared. Dink smiled at himself. Of course the car wasn't in the meadow—it was on River Road.

Dink slipped back into the barn, crawled into his sleeping bag, and closed his eyes.

Suddenly Polly started to whinny and Pal began barking.

"What's going on?" Josh asked

groggily. He switched on his flashlight and turned the beam on Polly.

"Look at her!" Ruth Rose said.

Polly's eyes were rolling in fright. She rose on her hind legs and kicked at her stall. Pal barked and ran over to Josh. "Something's been bugging them," Dink said. "They woke me up a little while ago."

Then all three kids smelled it.

"Smoke!" Josh yelled, kicking his way out of his sleeping bag.

The kids ran outside, expecting to see something burning. But the night was peaceful and dark.

Then Dink walked behind the barn. "Guys, over here!" he shouted.

Josh and Ruth Rose hurried around the corner. Dink pointed toward the river. A small orange blaze flickered in the night.

"There's a fire in the meadow!" Josh said.

CHAPTER 2

It took Green Lawn's fire truck only five minutes to get to the fire. Dink and Ruth Rose stood next to the barn. They watched with Josh and his family as the firefighters put out the blaze.

"I wanna go see the fire truck!" Josh's brother Bradley announced, wiggling in his father's arms.

"Afraid not," his dad said. "Besides, the fire's out, and you're going to bed."

"No, I wanna stay up!" Bradley's twin, Brian, complained. "It's time to play!"

Josh's dad just laughed.

Dink looked at his watch. It was about one-thirty. Across the meadow, he could see the fire truck's lights. The firefighters' voices sounded muffled.

A few minutes later, they saw the fire engine leaving. Soon the taillights disappeared on River Road. "Okay, the excitement's over," Josh's mother said, taking Brian's hand. "Back to bed, everyone."

"You three get some sleep," Josh's dad said as he carried Bradley toward the house.

"Okay, Dad," Josh said. The kids and Pal straggled into the barn. Pal flopped into the hay pile next to Polly again, and the kids climbed into their sleeping bags.

Suddenly Dink popped up. "Hey, guys, I just realized something. I may have seen who set the fire!" he said.

"What're you talking about?" Josh asked.

"Polly woke me up before we smelled the fire," Dink explained. "I went out to look around and saw headlights over by the river!"

"Maybe someone was camping," Ruth Rose said. She yawned. "We can check in the morning."

It's already morning, Dink thought, copying Ruth Rose's yawn. He lay back down. As he was falling asleep, he heard a scratchy sound in the dark.

He froze, imagining some night creature crawling over—or *into*—his sleeping bag.

Then he heard munching, and he smelled cookies.

"Josh!" Dink said. "You almost gave me a heart attack!"

"Sorry," Josh said, swallowing. "I was hungry!"

When the kids woke up, sunlight was streaming through the dusty barn window. Birds chirped. The kids kicked out of their sleeping bags and stepped into their sneakers.

"Let's go see that fire," Josh said. His clothes were wrinkled and his hair stood in spikes.

Pal gazed up at Josh with big brown eyes.

"Okay, you can come, too," he said, snapping Pal's leash onto his collar. Ruth Rose fed Polly a carrot, and then they left the barn.

The sun peeked through the trees as the kids hiked across the meadow. The tall grass was heavy with dew. Their sneakers and legs were soon soaked.

"Look!" Ruth Rose said. Straight ahead was a soggy pile of blackened wood. The air stunk of smoke and wet ashes.

The ground was even wetter here. There were still puddles from the firefighters' hoses. Dink noticed deep footprints in the mushy, trampled grass.

"Why would somebody light a fire here?" Josh asked, looking around. They were standing near the edge of River Road. On the other side of the road, a short bank dropped off to Indian River.

"Maybe they were roasting marshmallows," Ruth Rose said. She found a long stick and began poking the mess of charred wood and ash.

"In the middle of the night?" Josh asked. "Who eats then?"

Dink laughed. "You do, Mr. Cookie Monster."

Josh grinned.

"What's this?" Ruth Rose asked.

She picked up a hunk of wood and wiped it clean. It was about six inches long and three inches wide. Both ends were charred, but the middle hadn't been burned. Stamped into the board with black ink were the letters ET CO. "What's ET CO?" Josh asked.

"CO could be the first two letters of *Connecticut,*" Ruth Rose said.

"Or *Colorado,*" Dink added.

"I wonder if someone started the fire just to get rid of this," Ruth Rose said, examining the narrow piece of wood.

"It would be nice to know how many letters got burned off," Dink said. "ET CO could be part of lots of words, like *pet comb* or *wet coat.*"

"Or *sweet cotton candy,*" Josh added.

"The CO could be short for *corporation,*" Ruth Rose suggested, shoving the wood into her back pocket.

"I think it stands for *get cookies!*" Josh yelled. He started to run. "Last one back to the barn doesn't get any!"

CHAPTER 3

Josh burst through the barn doors first. Dink and Ruth Rose barreled in right behind him.

Josh immediately pounced on the cookie tin. He opened it, then gasped. "Call the cops!" he yelled. "I've been robbed!"

Dink grinned at his friend. "What'd they take, your brain?"

"Worse," Josh said, peering into the empty cookie tin. "They took my cookies!"

"Hey, my piggy bank is missing!"

Ruth Rose said. "I left it right on my sleeping bag."

Dink poked his hand into the opening of his sleeping bag. He felt around. "My money jar isn't here, either!" he said.

Josh pulled open his sleeping bag. "Now I'm *really* mad!" he said. "My money sock is gone!"

Josh looked at his friends. "Someone snuck in here while we were gone," he said.

"Raccoons might have taken the cookies," Ruth Rose said, glancing around the barn.

"And I read that crows sometimes steal shiny coins," Dink offered.

Suddenly Josh grinned. "No, it wasn't raccoons or crows," he said, wiggling his eyebrows. "I think it was two little monkeys!"

"The twins!" shouted Dink and Ruth Rose at the same time.

The three kids charged out of the barn and raced across the yard. Josh stormed through the kitchen door and yelled, "Freeze!"

Brian and Bradley were kneeling on kitchen chairs, playing with a pile of coins on the table. On the counter were Josh's blue sock, Dink's peanut butter jar, and Ruth Rose's piggy bank. "Josh!" cried Bradley. "Look what we found in the barn!"

"It's pirate treasure!" yelled Brian.

"No, it's not. It's *our* treasure," Josh growled at his little brothers.

Bradley made a face. "But we found it. Nobody was there!"

"This is special money," Dink told the twins. "We saved it for the ducks."

"Why do ducks need money?" asked Brian.

Ruth Rose explained how the money would be used to build a bridge so mommy ducks and baby ducks could cross the road safely.

"Okay," the twins said together.

"Now, what about my cookies?" Josh asked, waving the cookie tin. "Give 'em back!"

The two little boys erupted in giggles.

"We can't—they're in our stomachs!" Brian crowed.

The five kids ate breakfast, and then Josh told Bradley and Brian to go wake up their parents.

Dink scooped all their coins into the cookie tin while Josh and Ruth Rose cleaned up. Then Josh reached for Pal's leash. But Pal was already sitting by the door with his leash in his mouth.

"Smart doggie," Josh said as he clipped the leash to Pal's collar. Dink lugged the heavy cookie tin.

Pal and the kids took Eagle Lane to Silver Circle, then crossed Main Street to the fire station. They saw Officer Fallon getting out of his cruiser in front of the station.

"'Morning, kids," the police chief said. "You're up early." He bent down and stroked Pal's soft ears.

Dink held up the cookie tin. "We came to make a deposit!"

Officer Fallon grinned. He reached into his cruiser and pulled out a jar of coins. "Me too."

"Did you hear about the fire last night?" Ruth Rose asked.

"Yes, I did," Officer Fallon said. "It was small, and I guess the fire department put it out easily. The question is, who started it?"

"I saw a car's headlights near there," Dink reported. "But that was before the fire."

"How long before?" Officer Fallon asked.

Dink thought back. "I don't know, maybe ten minutes or so."

Officer Fallon set his coin jar on the roof of his cruiser. Then he pulled out his pad, flipped it open, and made a few notes.

"Could this be a clue?" Ruth Rose asked. She pulled the partly burned wood from her pocket.

"Where'd you find that, Ruth Rose?" he asked.

"We went to the scene of the fire this morning," she told him. "This was in the ashes."

Officer Fallon examined the four letters. "CO is usually short for *company*," he said, "but there should be a period after the O."

"Maybe the period got burned off?" Ruth Rose said.

Officer Fallon made a note on his pad. "Good detective work," he said to Ruth Rose.

Josh's eyes lit up. "Maybe the wood was from a snake's cage," he said. *"Don't pet cobra."*

They all laughed.

"Well, let's add our money so we

can save those ducks," Officer Fallon said, slipping his notebook into a pocket and reaching for his money jar.

They walked into the fire station together. Somewhere a radio played softly. A clock on the rear wall said nine o'clock.

The Green Lawn fire engine was parked on the concrete floor. Next to it was a smaller truck with RESCUE written on both doors.

On the back wall were three doors. Gray metal lockers stood along another wall. Below the lockers was a row of rubber boots. Pal walked over and sniffed a boot.

"Hello!" Officer Fallon called out. "Anybody home?"

One of the doors opened. A man wearing a dark blue uniform stepped out. "Who's there?" he said.

"Officer Fallon and some friends," the police chief said, rattling his jarful of coins. "We brought more money."

Dink held up the cookie tin. "This is getting heavy!" he said.

"Great!" the man said. "Come on back here."

The kids and Officer Fallon joined the man at the rear of the firehouse. The man walked over to another of the doors. He shoved it open and stepped aside. "Right in here," he said.

Through the door, Dink could see a rug, a TV set, and several comfortable-looking chairs.

"Where's the bank?" Josh asked, peering around the man.

"Standing in the corner, right where it's always been," the man said, turning to look into the room.

Except that the duck bank wasn't standing in the corner.

The duck bank wasn't anywhere in the room.

CHAPTER 4

"I can't believe it!" the man said. "That bank was here last night. I know because I put money in it!"

"Would anyone have moved it to a different spot in the firehouse?" Officer Fallon asked.

The man shook his head. "We kept it here in the TV lounge so everyone would be reminded to drop coins in. Plus, the thing weighs a ton!"

Officer Fallon handed Josh his jar of coins and took out a notebook. "Did you put out that meadow fire last night?" he asked.

The man shook his head. "Nope, that would've been Jake and Lenny."

Officer Fallon wrote in his notebook. "Where would I find them?"

The firefighter smiled. "Still snoozing in the other room," he said. "They should be getting up any time now."

"Have them give me a call after they're awake," Officer Fallon said, slipping his notebook into a pocket.

"No problem," the man answered.

Officer Fallon and the kids walked outside. Pal lay next to the cruiser with his head on his big front paws.

"I just thought of something," Dink said. "Maybe whoever lit that fire last night did it to get the men out of the firehouse."

"I had the same thought," Officer Fallon said. "The fire could have been a diversion."

"Yeah!" Josh said. "So they could

sneak in here when no one was around and steal the bank!"

"Who would do such a lousy thing?" Ruth Rose said.

"Someone who loves money and hates ducks!" Josh said.

"Could it have been the car I saw last night?" Dink said. "I saw those headlights right before the fire."

"Very possibly," Officer Fallon said.

An elderly man walked past with a dog on a leash. The man was tall and thin. The dog was short and round. They both had white hair. Pal whined and wagged his tail back and forth.

The man let his little dog waddle over to Pal. "Hello," the man said. "This is Randolph. Is your basset friendly?"

Josh nodded. "Pal likes everyone!"

Pal sniffed the little dog, then licked his face. Randolph rolled over and wiggled his whole body.

"Any trouble here?" the man asked, looking curiously at Officer Fallon.

"Just investigating a possible theft," Officer Fallon said.

The man raised his bushy white eyebrows. "Would it have anything to do with that crazy driver I saw last night?" he asked.

Officer Fallon took out his notebook again and flipped it open. "Please tell me what you saw," he said.

"A fire engine woke me some time after one o'clock," the man said. "So I took Randolph outside for some fresh air. We were at the corner of Indian Way Road when a jeep came tearing past us up Main Street!" The man held his hands a foot apart. "Missed Randolph by that much!"

Officer Fallon began writing in his notebook. "You are Mr. . . . ?"

"Thaddeus Pocket," the man said. "Number 10 Indian Way Road."

"Were you able to read the jeep's license plate, Mr. Pocket?"

"Mercy, no!" the man said. "It was speeding much too fast."

"Did you happen to notice the driver?" Officer Fallon asked.

Mr. Pocket shook his head. "I'm sorry, my eyesight isn't wonderful anymore. There were two men in the jeep, but I don't remember the driver."

Officer Fallon closed his notebook and began to put it away. "Thanks anyway, Mr. Pocket. You've been very helpful—"

"But I do remember the man sitting *beside* the driver," Mr. Pocket went on.

"You do?" Officer Fallon opened his notebook again.

Mr. Pocket grinned. "Yes, but only because he was so odd-looking. The man in the passenger seat looked just like a giant duck!"

CHAPTER 5

Dink, Josh, and Ruth Rose exchanged glances.

Officer Fallon was still looking at Mr. Pocket. "The man looked like a duck? Can you explain, Mr. Pocket?"

Mr. Pocket smiled. "I noticed a shiny head and a duck's beak. Now I realize the man must have had a shaved head and a large nose."

Officer Fallon thanked Mr. Pocket and wrote down his phone number. The man and his dog continued their walk.

"That guy driving the jeep must have

been the thief!" Josh blurted out. "The duck bank was in the passenger seat!"

"When Mr. Pocket saw the jeep, the driver had probably just stolen the bank and was making his getaway!" Ruth Rose added.

Officer Fallon walked over to his cruiser. "I'll get word out to watch for a jeep carrying a duck," he said.

"Would you mind holding on to our money?" Dink asked. He stepped over to the cruiser and handed Officer Fallon the cookie tin.

"And here's yours back." Josh returned Officer Fallon's jar.

"Will do," Officer Fallon said, setting both containers on the seat. "Don't worry, we'll get our duck bridge built yet."

He climbed into the car and pulled away down Main Street.

"That crook could be anywhere by

now," Dink said. He started walking toward the corner of Main and River Road.

"It makes me so mad!" Ruth Rose said. "The town has been saving up for a year, and now we have to start all over again!"

The kids crossed River Road and sat in the grass above the riverbank. Pal woofed at a family of ducks feeding in the weeds. The ducks paddled quickly away toward the other side.

"Maybe Officer Fallon will find him," Dink said.

"I don't know how," Josh said. "That jeep could be hundreds of miles away by now."

"Well, we still have this," Ruth Rose said, holding up the chunk of wood stamped with ET CO. "These letters *must* mean something!"

Josh picked up a stone and tossed it into the river. The kids watched the stone sink to the sandy bottom.

"Any ideas?" Dink asked.

"Yeah, let's go to Ellie's," Josh said. "A milkshake always helps me think better."

"Josh, we have to focus on finding that money," Ruth Rose said. "Think of those baby ducks!"

"Okay, but we don't have a plan," Josh said.

Dink checked his watch. "Why don't we see if the firemen who were on duty last night are up yet?" he suggested.

"Good idea," Ruth Rose said. "Maybe they saw the jeep when they were coming back from the fire."

With Pal leading, the kids walked back into the fire station. A tall man was wiping the rescue truck with a cloth. A mug of coffee rested on the truck's hood.

"'Morning," he said, yawning.

"Good morning," Dink said. "Are you one of the night firemen?"

"Did you hear about the robbery?" Josh asked before the man could answer Dink's question.

The man nodded. "My name's Jake," he said. "I'm really bummed that someone stole that duck money."

He picked up his coffee and sat on the truck's front bumper. "Lenny and I were gone, putting out a fire in the meadow. It turned out to be small, probably left burning by some campers."

"Officer Fallon thinks the crooks set it," Josh said.

"We figure they did it to get you to leave the firehouse," Dink said. "I saw some headlights near where the fire was set last night."

"And a man walking his dog saw a jeep speeding up Main Street," Ruth Rose added. "He saw the duck bank in the jeep!"

Jake's mouth fell open. "Really?"

"By any chance, did you pass a jeep on River Road?" Josh asked.

Jake shook his head. "Didn't see any

vehicles, going or coming back."

"Did you see anyone hanging around here?" Ruth Rose asked.

Jake leaned down and gave Pal's ears a gentle rub. "Not last night, but a few days ago some guy was poking around in here. He used our bathroom, then left."

"Did he see the duck bank?" Dink asked.

"Probably. The thing's pretty hard to miss," Jake said.

"Do you remember what he looked like?" Josh asked.

Jake shrugged. "Big guy, as tall as me but heavier," he said. "Oh, and his ears really stuck out. Looked like he had two overgrown mushrooms glued to his head."

CHAPTER 6

The kids thanked Jake and left.

"That guy could have been the robber!" Ruth Rose said.

"I think so, too," Dink said. "The thief would have to be big to carry that duck filled with coins."

"Now can I get a milkshake?" Josh asked. "Please? I'm starving!"

"If you promise not to slurp and embarrass us," Dink said.

With Pal tugging on his leash, they walked to Ellie's Diner. They sat in a booth by the windows. Pal crawled under the table and rested his head on Josh's feet.

"Hi, kids," Ellie said. She brought Pal a bowl of water and patted him on the head.

Then she pulled out her pad. "What'll it be? Our specials are slug stew and spider spaghetti."

"Yum," Ruth Rose said, "but Josh simply *has* to have a milkshake." She pulled the ET CO wood from her back pocket and laid it on the table.

"What's that?" asked Ellie.

"It's a clue," Ruth Rose said. "Did you hear about the duck bank? It got stolen last night!"

"Go on!" Ellie said. She sat next to Dink. "Tell me everything!"

The kids told Ellie about the fire, the speeding jeep, and what they'd learned from Jake at the firehouse.

"This came from the fire," Ruth

Rose said, touching the chunk of wood. "We've been trying to figure out what ET CO stands for."

Ellie picked up the wood and examined the letters. Suddenly she smiled and handed it back to Ruth Rose. "Well, that part of the mystery I can solve. Come on out back," she said.

"Stay," Josh told Pal. Then the kids followed Ellie behind the counter, through the kitchen, and out the back door.

Ellie walked over to a small wooden platform lying on the ground. It was made of narrow boards that had been nailed across thicker ones.

"I've seen those before," Josh said. "When my dad ordered a bunch of bricks, they came loaded on one of these things."

"It's called a pallet," Ellie said.

"Look!" Ruth Rose said. She pointed

to words stamped into the pallet boards: EASTERN PALLET COMPANY.

Ruth Rose held her partly burned piece of wood next to the words. The black printing was identical.

"Where do they make these things?" Dink asked.

"Beats me," Ellie said. "This one came from the supermarket. I'm using the wood to build a fence around my garden."

"Could anyone get one?" Ruth Rose asked.

Ellie shrugged. "I guess. I talked to the store manager, a guy named Derek Robb. So do you still want milkshakes?"

"Yes!" Josh said. He led the way back into the diner.

The kids gave Ellie their orders, then slid back into the booth.

Ruth Rose leaned toward Dink and Josh. "I'll bet the crook used pallets from the supermarket to start the fire!" she said.

"If he did, maybe Derek Robb remembers him!" Dink said.

"So let's go ask," Ruth Rose suggested.

"Can we *please* drink our milkshakes first?" Josh asked.

CHAPTER 7

After the kids had finished their milkshakes, they left Ellie's and walked back up Main Street to Green Lawn's supermarket.

Josh tied Pal's leash to a bike rack. "We'll be right back," he told his dog.

Inside, Dink, Josh, and Ruth Rose walked through the fruit and vegetable section. Tall pyramids of oranges and apples gleamed under the lights.

They stood next to a mountain of watermelons and glanced around the store. A lot of people were shopping, and a lot of workers were scurrying about. All the store employees wore dark pants, green aprons, and white shirts.

Dink walked over to a woman with curly brown hair. She was arranging bags of grapes into a display. A name tag pinned to her apron said HI! I'M JUDY.

Dink asked her where the manager's office was.

"Go to the rear of the store," Judy said, pointing. "It's the red door just left of the meat department."

The kids followed her directions, and Dink knocked on the door.

"Come in!" a voice boomed.

Ruth Rose opened the door and the kids walked in. The office was cluttered with filing cabinets, boxes of damaged canned goods, and a wooden desk covered with papers.

Behind the desk sat a smiling man in a shirt and tie. DEREK ROBB was printed on a nameplate on his desk.

DEREK ROBB

"Hi there," the man said. "How can I help you kids?"

"Someone set a fire in the meadow behind my barn last night," Josh said. "We think whoever set it used pallets from this store."

Ruth Rose showed Mr. Robb the chunk of burned wood.

Mr. Robb examined the letters ET CO. "Yep, looks the same," he said. "A lot of our merchandise comes stacked on these things."

"Did you give any pallets to a tall

man a couple of days ago?" Dink asked.

Mr. Robb smiled. "People who want pallets usually just take them," he said. "Come on, I'll show you."

Mr. Robb led the kids out of his office. They passed a long wall covered with framed photographs of employees. Dink recognized Judy, the woman who'd given him directions.

"Right through here," Mr. Robb said, pushing through a wide pair of swinging doors. "Watch out for the forklifts!"

The kids found themselves in a giant room filled with workers, boxes, and noise. Men and women were unpacking crates and loading stuff on carts.

"Look," Josh said. A yellow forklift stopped near a bunch of boxes stacked on a pallet. The driver pulled a lever, and the forklift's two arms lowered. The truck moved forward, and the arms slid under the pallet. The driver moved the lever again, and the arms raised the pallet of boxes off the floor.

Suddenly the forklift began to back up, beeping. The kids and Mr. Robb stepped back as the forklift carried the pallet to the other end of the room.

"Cool!" Josh said. "I wish I had one of those things."

Mr. Robb chuckled. "They're pretty expensive, kiddo. Now follow me." He led the kids to a tall, wide opening like a garage door.

"If you go down those steps," Mr. Robb said, pointing, "you'll see a stack of pallets on the ground. Folks stop by and take them all the time. They break 'em up for firewood, whatever."

"So anyone could just come and take one," Dink said, "at any time?"

"That's right," said Mr. Robb. "Even in the middle of the night."

CHAPTER 8

"Well, at least we know where the thief got the wood for the fire," Ruth Rose said.

The kids were outside again, standing between the supermarket and the fire station.

"So where did the guy take the duck bank in his jeep?" Josh asked. "Mr. Pocket said he was on Main Street, but we don't know which direction he was going."

"Yes, we do," Ruth Rose said.

Josh looked at her. "Ruth Rose, the

guy could have been heading north or south."

Ruth Rose shook her head. "He couldn't have been heading south," she said. "Mr. Pocket told us the jeep passed him on the corner of Indian Way Road. If it was coming from the fire station, the jeep had to be going north."

"She's right," Dink said. "And north is toward River Road."

Josh looked in that direction. "So when he got to River Road, he either turned right toward Blue Hills, or left toward Hartford."

"Let's go talk to Mr. Pocket," Ruth Rose suggested. "He might remember which way the jeep turned."

"Where do we find him?" Dink asked.

"He lives at number 10 Indian Way Road," Ruth Rose said.

Josh laughed and shook his head.

"How can you remember stuff like that?" he asked.

Ruth Rose just smiled.

The kids collected Pal from the bike rack, and then they cut behind the fire station to Indian Way Road.

Number 10 was a small gray-shingled house behind a white fence. Rosebushes filled the yard and drooped over the fence. A stone path led from the gate to the porch, where Mr. Pocket was sitting in a rocking chair. Randolph was on his lap.

"Well, hello again," the elderly man called out.

"Hi," Dink said, standing at the gate. "We had some questions about the jeep you saw last night. Could we talk to you?"

"Of course," Mr. Pocket said. "Come on in! Mind the roses—those thorns love arms and legs!"

Dink opened the gate and the kids stepped through.

"Would you mind closing it behind you?" Mr. Pocket called. "Randolph thinks he can go exploring without me!"

Ruth Rose smiled at Mr. Pocket. She pulled the gate shut and made sure the latch snapped into place.

The kids walked carefully past the rosebushes and joined Mr. Pocket on his porch. Pal looked up at Randolph and wagged his tail.

"Okay, Randolph, you can visit your friend," Mr. Pocket said. He set his dog on the porch near Pal.

Then he stood and removed a bunch of newspapers from a long bench. "Please sit," he told the kids.

The kids lined up on the bench and Mr. Pocket dropped back into his chair.

A pair of eyeglasses lay on a low table next to the chair. Mr. Pocket put on his glasses and smiled at the kids. "Now, please tell me what's going on," he said. "Why all the interest in this jeep?"

The kids told Mr. Pocket about the money being collected, the fire, and the theft of the duck bank.

"That wasn't a passenger you saw in the seat next to the driver," Dink said. "It was the duck bank."

"Well, I'll be pickled!" Mr. Pocket said. "I remember thinking it was strange how the moon reflected off his face. And all the time, it was a plastic duck!"

"Um, you wouldn't happen to know which way he turned on River Road?" Dink said. "Did he have a blinker on?"

Mr. Pocket shook his head. "Nope. Didn't have any lights on at all. That's why I didn't see him till he almost ran over my toes!"

Mr. Pocket leaned forward. "And if
you want my opinion, the driver never
meant to turn on River Road," he said. "I
truly believe he aimed his jeep straight
for the river!"

Dink gulped. "Right into the water?"
he said.

The old man nodded. "Yep. Unless
that jeep knew how to fly."

"That would explain why the guys in

the fire truck didn't pass the jeep,"
Dink said.

"I'd like to make a donation for your duck bridge," Mr. Pocket said. He fished a small leather pouch from his pocket and took out four quarters. He leaned over and handed them to Josh. "Always liked ducks."

"Thanks a lot, sir," Josh said as he accepted the money. "If we find the bank, I'll put it in for you."

The kids and Pal left Mr. Pocket sitting on his porch with his dog. They walked to the corner of Main, then turned left and headed for the river.

Between the edge of River Road and the water, there was a patch of weeds. Some of them were crushed flat, lying toward the river.

When the kids were close enough, they realized that there were actually two flattened strips, side by side.

Josh bent over the smashed grass.

"They sure look like tire tracks to me," he said. "Mr. Pocket was right!"

Dink, Josh, and Ruth Rose sat and looked out over the river. Pal put his front feet in the river and began lapping up water. Josh held the leash so Pal couldn't go out any farther.

"Could the jeep drive right across the river?" Ruth Rose asked.

"Sure," Josh said. "On TV I've seen guys in jeeps plow right through water deeper than this."

"We should go look on the other side for more tracks," Dink said.

Josh frowned. "But how do we—"

"Look," Dink interrupted, pointing to a flat-bottomed rowboat coming down the river. The man rowing the boat seemed too big for it, like a grown-up sitting on a kid's bike. The man rowed slowly, peering over the sides into the water as he moved.

The boat slowed, then stopped. The

man removed one of the oars from the oarlock. He began poking the oar into the water. He did it several times, on both sides of the boat.

Then the man set the oar back into the oarlock. He stretched a long arm into the water. He paused a moment, then suddenly laughed.

The man splashed some water onto his face and head. He shook his hair like a wet dog, grabbed both oars, and began rowing for the opposite shore.

When he reached land, he got out and dragged the boat behind him. The man and the boat disappeared into the trees.

"Did you see how big that guy was?" Dink asked.

"Not only that," Josh said. "Did you notice his ears? Mushrooms!"

CHAPTER 9

"That was the thief!" Ruth Rose said.

"But what was he looking for?" Dink asked.

"Maybe the bank fell out of the jeep when it was crossing," Ruth Rose suggested.

"That duck is pretty big," Josh said. "Wouldn't he be able to see it just lying in the water?"

"Well, he found *something*," Ruth Rose said.

"And I'm going to find out what," Josh said. He looped Pal's leash around

a tree, pulled off his sneakers, and started wading into the river.

"Wait for me!" Dink said, yanking off his own sneakers.

"I'm coming, too!" said Ruth Rose, kicking off her sandals.

They pushed their feet through the warm, shallow water. Dink could feel the fine sand between his toes. The water was so clear he could see the tiny pebbles on the bottom.

"It's getting kind of muddy," Josh said, a few yards ahead of Dink.

Suddenly Josh stopped. He turned around with panic on his face. "I'm stuck!" he cried.

As Dink watched, Josh started to sink. The water was up to his knees!

"I can't pull my feet out!" Josh yelled. "I think it's quicksand!"

"Wait a minute!" Dink said. He lunged ahead and grabbed Josh's arm.

Then Dink felt the sand closing over his own feet and his ankles, climbing steadily to his knees. He was stuck, too!

"Ruth Rose!" Dink shouted. "Don't come any closer!"

"I'll run for help!" Ruth Rose yelled. She turned and splashed back to shore.

Dink watched her climb the bank and race across River Road in her bare feet. Pal was straining on his leash and barking.

Josh pulled out of Dink's grasp, struggling to walk back toward the edge. But the more he struggled, the deeper he sank.

"Don't move!" Dink yelled. "Get on your back."

To demonstrate, Dink fell backward into the water. He floated on his back, facing up. His legs were still stuck, but at least he wasn't sinking.

"Do it—it works!" he called to Josh.

Dink heard a splash as Josh fell over

into the water. He could hear his own heart pounding in his ears. Trying to calm himself, he closed his eyes and let his body float.

Suddenly Pal began to bark even more wildly. Turning his head, Dink saw Jake and another man running toward the river carrying a ladder. Ruth Rose was right behind them.

At the river's edge, the men flopped the ladder into the water.

"Don't move!" Jake yelled out to Dink and Josh. "Just stay the way you are. Lenny and I will have you out in a jiffy."

The firefighters shoved the ladder out into the water toward Dink. When it was near enough, he grabbed the last rung.

"Hold on, kid!" Jake yelled.

The men pulled the ladder. Dink could feel suction on his legs, as if the quicksand didn't want to let him go.

But Jake and Lenny were stronger than the quicksand. Suddenly Dink's legs oozed free of the muck. When Dink's feet touched solid river bottom, he splashed ashore.

Immediately, the men thrust the ladder back out over the river. Jake waded in and pushed the ladder until Josh could grab a rung. Pulling the ladder hand over hand, he and Lenny hauled Josh out of the river like a fish. Dink and Josh sat side by side, catching their breath. They were both sopping wet and red-faced. Pal lapped Josh's face

and jumped all over his muddy legs. "Don't ever do that again!" Ruth Rose said.

"Don't worry," Josh said. "I'm never even taking a *bath* again!"

Everyone burst out laughing.

"By the way," Jake said, slapping the other man on the back, "this is Lenny."

Lenny smiled at the kids. "Glad to meet you," he said.

"Not as glad as *we* are," Dink said, standing up to shake Lenny's hand.

"What were you kids doing out there?" Lenny asked.

"That's where the jeep is!" Josh said.

"It is?" Dink asked. "Josh, we don't know—"

"It's there," Josh said, pulling on his sneakers. "When I was lying in the water, something sharp stuck me in the leg. I reached down and felt the jeep's antenna! That must be what that guy in the boat found!"

"We have to go get Officer Fallon," Ruth Rose said.

"No need to," Jake said, holding a hand in the air. "I called him from the station. Listen."

They heard a siren coming closer. Twenty seconds later, a cruiser roared up to the river and stopped. Officer Fallon jumped out and practically slid into the river in his haste.

"You kids all right?" he said, looking from one face to the other.

"We're fine," Dink said. "And Josh found the crook's jeep!"

"You did? Where?"

Josh pointed out into the water. "Out there, buried in quicksand."

"I never even knew there was quicksand in Connecticut," Ruth Rose said.

"Quicksand can be anywhere there's water and sand," Lenny said. "I was a Navy SEAL, and I saw plenty of the stuff."

"But we've waded in the river lots of times," Josh said. "I never got stuck before."

"Sometimes you find it only in small pockets," Lenny explained. "In fact, right here is a perfect spot for it. Lots of sand under shallow, slow-moving water."

"But how did you know to look here?" Officer Fallon asked the kids.

"We went to see Mr. Pocket," Dink

explained. "He told us it seemed like the jeep went straight instead of turning on River Road. So we came here and found tire tracks."

"Then we saw a guy in a boat," Josh added. "He was looking for something in the water. He found it, then took off."

"That's when Josh decided to take a mud bath," Ruth Rose said with a grin.

The three men and three kids looked out over the river. The blue sky, sparkling water, and golden sand looked so peaceful.

"If you're right about the jeep," Officer Fallon said, "the duck bank is probably down there, too."

"But how can we get it out?" Ruth Rose asked.

Officer Fallon scratched his chin. "That's a good question," he said.

"I think I have the answer," Lenny said.

CHAPTER 10

Everyone looked at Lenny.

"Quicksand is just a kind of soup made of sand and water," he explained. "Beneath the quicksand there's a layer of hard clay or rock. The quicksand lies on top of that hard stuff because it can't drain out."

"But how far down is the hard layer?" Officer Fallon asked.

"The only way to find out is to get out there in the stuff," Lenny said. "But if these kids found the antenna sticking up, the jeep must be just beneath the surface of sand."

"So we'll get a hook on that baby and pull it out, right, Lenny?" Jake asked.

"Yeah, if I can find the bumper," Lenny said. "I'll go out there and see what's what. You go back to the firehouse and get the truck."

Twenty minutes later, everything was in place. Jake had backed the rescue truck to the riverbank. A long cable with a big hook on one end lay on the ground. The other end snaked into the winch on the back of the truck.

Standing at the water's edge, Lenny held the hook end of the cable.

"Okay," Jake called to Lenny. "Go fishing!"

Dragging the cable and hook, Lenny half floated, half swam out into the river. Dink, Josh, and Ruth Rose hunkered down under a tree and watched. Pal's head was resting on Josh's knees.

Officer Fallon sat in his cruiser, talking into his car phone.

A small crowd of people stood watching on the edge of River Road.

"I sure hope the duck bank is still in the jeep," Dink said.

"And I hope Lenny doesn't get stuck in the quicksand," Josh added.

"Okay, I think I'm right over the rear of the jeep," Lenny yelled. He took a deep breath and plunged under the water.

A minute passed. Everyone stared at the spot where Lenny had disappeared. Dink glanced at his watch.

"The quicksand must have him!" Josh yelled.

"Let's not panic," Jake said. "If he gets in trouble, we'll haul him out by the cable." But Jake looked worried.

Suddenly the surface of the water erupted. Lenny popped up like a cork on a fishing line. He began spitting and shaking mud from his arms and shoulders.

"What took you so long?" Jake yelled to his partner.

"The jeep sank at an angle," Lenny called back. "So unfortunately, the bumper is lower down than I thought."

"Did you get the hook on it?" Jake asked.

Lenny grinned. "Of course I did! Pull her in, Jake!"

Jake ran to the truck and threw a lever, and the cable began to inch backward into the winch. As the cable tightened, the winch strained, making a noise like fingernails on a chalkboard. Everybody stared at the river.

Out in the water, the back end of a yellow jeep suddenly broke the surface.

"There it is!" Ruth Rose cried.

Officer Fallon had come to stand behind the kids. "Well, I'll be darned," he muttered.

They all heard a sucking sound as the quicksand gave up the jeep. Inch by inch, the jeep oozed toward the riverbank like some yellow sea monster. Water and sand cascaded off the metal and glass.

Finally, the jeep's rear tires came to rest against the riverbank. In the passenger seat, wet and muddy, sat the duck bank. The coins were barely visible through the clear plastic because of the sand and water that had seeped in.

"This bank must weigh a ton with all that water and muck inside," Lenny said. "I know I can't lift it."

"Let's haul the jeep back to the firehouse," Jake suggested. He climbed into the driver's seat of the rescue truck. "We'll use the hoist to lift the bank, then empty out the money and let it dry."

"And I'd like to see what's in that glove compartment," Officer Fallon said.

Lenny nodded. He opened the jeep's doors, letting muddy water flood out onto the ground. With it came a soggy mixture of old hamburger wrappers, a T-shirt, and a ragged green towel.

"Okay," Lenny said. "Take 'er away."

The rescue truck slowly pulled the jeep toward the firehouse. Water was still oozing out. Officer Fallon followed in his cruiser. With the excitement over, people began to wander away.

"Let's go watch them empty out the bank," Dink said.

"Could we get some lunch first?" Josh asked as he untied Pal's leash from the tree. "I swear I'm losing weight here."

"Okay, we can go to my house and eat," Ruth Rose said. "I wouldn't want Josh to get any skinnier."

Pal was sniffing the wet hamburger wrappers that had just poured out of the jeep.

"See, even my dog is hungry," Josh teased.

"Wait a minute, guys," Ruth Rose said. Using the toe of her sandal, she kicked at the wet towel.

Only it wasn't a towel. It was a green apron. And flashing in the sun was a name tag, pinned to the material.

Three words were printed on the name tag: HI! I'M MARTIN.

CHAPTER 11

The kids stood looking down at the name tag.

"I've seen an apron and name tag like this before," Dink said. "In the supermarket!"

"Martin must *work* there!" Josh said. "Let's go arrest him!"

"We can't arrest anybody," Ruth Rose said. "We have to tell Officer Fallon!"

Ruth Rose scooped up the apron and wrung out the water. Then the kids raced up the grassy slope and across River Road. Pal loped alongside Josh.

On the firehouse driveway, they saw Jake, Lenny, and a couple of other firefighters. The jeep was standing in a puddle of river water.

"Have you seen Officer Fallon?" Dink asked one of the firefighters.

"You just missed him," the man said, pointing to the jeep's open glove compartment. "He grabbed some papers and left."

"Do you know if he went to the police station?" Ruth Rose asked.

The firefighter shrugged. "He didn't say."

Dink looked at Josh and Ruth Rose. "What should we do?" he asked.

"If Martin is the crook, we need to let Officer Fallon know," Ruth Rose said.

"But it might be too late," Josh said. "If Martin works next door, he might have seen the jeep being dragged over here."

Josh quickly glanced toward the

supermarket. "He could be watching us right now!"

Dink thought for a minute. "We saw Martin in a rowboat a while ago, so maybe he isn't working at the market today," he said. "He might not know we found the jeep."

Ruth Rose was still holding the damp apron. She looked across the lawn toward the supermarket. "Come on," she said. "If Martin isn't working today, maybe we can find out where he lives. And even if he is working, we'll tell Officer Fallon."

They crossed the lawn that separated the fire station from the supermarket. Josh left Pal tied to the bike rack again, and the kids hurried inside.

"Keep your eyes peeled for a big guy with mushroom ears," Josh whispered.

But the store was packed with

Sunday shoppers. Dozens of workers in green aprons scurried around. Many of the male employees were pretty big.

"How will we ever find him?" Ruth Rose asked. "Martin could be anywhere!"

"I have an idea," Dink said. "When we were here before, I saw a bunch of pictures of employees. Let's check 'em out."

Josh and Ruth Rose followed Dink toward the back of the store. They cut through the pet food aisle, took a right at the dairy department, and stopped in front of the wall of photographs.

"There he is," Dink said, pointing. The man they'd seen in the rowboat was in the bottom row of pictures. He was the only one with huge ears.

"Martin Fleece," Dink said, reading the name under the picture.

"What should we do?" Josh asked.

Ruth Rose held up the apron. "We have to find out if he's here," she said. "Let's see if Mr. Robb is in his office."

The store manager's office was only a few yards from the wall of pictures. The door was open, and Dink could hear Mr. Robb's voice.

"Someone's in there with him," Dink whispered to Josh and Ruth Rose. They stood just outside the door.

"Marty, I just don't understand," Mr. Robb was saying. "Yesterday you were happy to work here, and today you want to quit."

"I'm sorry," a deep voice responded.

"But I have to go out of town. My . . . my grandmother is in the hospital, so I have to leave today. And I'll need my paycheck, too."

Josh peeked around the corner. When he looked back at Dink and Ruth Rose, his eyes were huge. "Martin Fleece!" he whispered.

"What can we do?" Ruth Rose asked.

"Let us take it from here," a quiet voice said, this time from behind Ruth Rose.

It was Officer Fallon with Officer Keene. "Did this come from the jeep?" Officer Fallon asked, pointing at the wet apron.

Ruth Rose nodded.

He took the apron and walked into Mr. Robb's office. Officer Keene followed and closed the door.

Dink, Josh, and Ruth Rose stepped closer and listened.

"Martin Fleece, you are under arrest

for theft," they heard Officer Fallon say.

One hour later, the kids were sitting in Officer Fallon's office. Martin Fleece was in jail.

"How did you know where to find him?" Dink asked Officer Fallon.

"The jeep's registration was in the glove compartment," Officer Fallon said. "His name and address were on it. One phone call told me he worked in the supermarket."

"How come he didn't get caught in the quicksand like I did?" Josh asked.

Officer Fallon shrugged. "Most likely, when the jeep got stuck, he realized he was in some kind of deep mud. He must have leapt clear, or swum till he could walk out of the river."

"Did the firefighters open the bank yet?" Ruth Rose asked.

Officer Fallon stood up. He opened his drawer and took out the cookie tin and his jar of money. "Why don't we go find out?" he asked.

Three weeks later, the duck bridge was completed. The high school kids had done a great job. The bridge was wooden and looked like a regular bridge, only it was much narrower than most. A small sign said DUCKS WELCOME.

One end of the bridge was on the riverbank, and it curved gracefully over River Road. Cars would be able to pass under it, and the ducks would be safe.

The town decided to have a grand opening the day after the bridge was finished. Dink, Josh, and Ruth Rose packed a picnic lunch. With Pal, the twins, and Ruth Rose's brother, Nate, they headed to the new duck bridge.

Officer Fallon was there with his grandson, Jimmy. Jake and Lenny both showed up, and Dink noticed Mr.

Pocket and Randolph.

While Nate, Brian, and Bradley kept Pal off the bridge, Ruth Rose unfolded a blanket. She looked for a flat place to spread it.

"Can you hurry it up, Ruth Rose?" Josh said. "Those sandwiches are calling me!"

"You *could* help out, Josh," Dink said. He grabbed one end of the blanket from Ruth Rose and helped her spread it. Then he opened the picnic basket.

Pal and the three little kids came running when they saw the sandwiches, cookies, and watermelon slices.

As the kids ate their lunch, the girl who had first suggested the bridge sprinkled cracked corn all along it. Everybody waited.

Some little kids began running around, playing tag. People started to chat with each other. Someone turned on a radio, and two big kids with a

Frisbee tossed it back and forth.

"Too much noise," Josh muttered. "It's like a party. A duck would have to be crazy to cross that bridge."

Gradually, everyone else got tired of waiting and went home.

"Where are the ducks?" Nate asked Ruth Rose.

"Maybe now that it's quieter, we'll see them," she whispered.

"Okay, we'll be *real* quiet!" Brian said. "Be quiet, Bradley!"

"I'm not talking!" Bradley argued. "*You* be quiet!"

Josh pulled his two brothers close to him. "If you want to see the ducks, you have to be as quiet as Pal," he whispered.

Pal was lying on the blanket, sound asleep. Nate, Brian, and Bradley flopped down on both sides of the dog. They cuddled up to him like puppies.

"Good move," Ruth Rose told Josh.

"Think the ducks will really come?" Dink whispered.

"They better," Josh mumbled. "After I nearly drowned for them!"

The six kids waited all afternoon. The little ones fell asleep. Dink, Josh, and Ruth Rose played Monopoly. Pal snored peacefully between the twins.

Josh was just about to land on

Dink's hotel when Ruth Rose whispered, "Look!"

A duck stood at the very top of the curved bridge. She turned her head in all directions, as if looking for danger. Seeing none, she quacked quietly. Five little yellow ducks waddled up to her.

Dink leaned over and woke Nate, Brian, and Bradley. Then they all sat like statues and watched the ducks cross safely over River Road.

Collect clues with Dink, Josh, and Ruth Rose in their next exciting adventure,

THE RUNAWAY RACEHORSE

Just then the door burst open. A blond woman in jeans and riding boots rushed into the kitchen.

"Hi, Sunny," Forest said. "Say hello to Dink, Josh, and Ruth Rose. They're here to watch you and Whirlaway win tomorrow."

"He's run away!" Sunny said, trying to catch her breath.

"Who's run away?"

"Whirlaway!" she said. "I found his stall door open—and he's gone!"

About the Author

Ron Roy is the author of more than thirty-five books for children, including *A Thousand Pails of Water*, *Where's Buddy?*, and the award-winning *Whose Hat Is That?* When he's not writing a thrilling new story for the A to Z Mysteries® series, Ron spends time traveling all over the country and restoring his old Connecticut farmhouse.